PETUNIA, I LOVE YOU

WRITTEN AND ILLUSTRATED BY

Roger Duvoisin

ALFRED · A · KNOPF : NEW YORK

To Danielle

L.C. Catalog card number: 65-21559

This is a Borzoi Book. Published by Alfred A. Knopf, Inc.

Copyright © 1965 by Roger Duvoisin.

Petunia did not know it,
but Raccoon thought of her every day,
and dreamed of her every night.
"How I long for Petunia," he sighed, "so handsome and so fat.
To think that I waste my time hunting mice and grasshoppers,
when I could feast like a king on a goose."

But what could he do? Petunia was stronger than Raccoon.
A blow from her wing had put to flight bigger animals than he.

Raccoon's dreams had made him so hungry
that he went to Petunia's barnyard one morning,
at a time when all raccoons are asleep in their tree holes.

"Dear Petunia," said Raccoon, who had thought of a wicked scheme,
"you are so pretty. I love you, Petunia.
It would make me so happy just to have your company
for a little walk in the forest.
Today, I am going to see my old aunt. Won't you come along?"
"You are so polite and kind, Raccoon," said Petunia.

"It would be rude of me to refuse. Pray, lead the way."
"To you the honor, dear Petunia. I'll walk behind you."
"If we walked side by side," said Petunia,
"it would make conversation more pleasant."
"As you will, lovely Petunia," agreed Raccoon.
"Let us be patient," he thought to himself.
"I can best trap her once we are in the forest."

Chatting and walking side by side,
Petunia and Raccoon came to a wide stream
which was bridged by a fallen tree.

"We shall cross on that tree, one behind the other," said Raccoon.
"You shall not wet your feathers, nor I my fur. After you, please."
"All goes well," he thought, as he followed Petunia.
"In the middle of the log, I will jump on her neck and . . . ."

But the tree, too rotten for their weight, broke in two
and crashed into the stream.
Petunia, with two beats of her wings, flew to the bank
while Raccoon fell in the water with a splash.

Petunia giggled when Raccoon climbed back to the bank, dripping wet.
"Please don't mind my laughing, poor dear Raccoon," she said.
"But I never saw a dripping raccoon, and that's very funny."
"Not funnier than a giggling goose," grumbled Raccoon.
"Let's go on with our walk."
They were soon in the deepest part of the forest
where stood the old oak tree with holes in its trunk.
"Is this where your aunt lives?" asked Petunia.
"Why, no," answered Raccoon. "It's the magic tree of the forest.
When you put your head into the bottom hole,
you see the other side of the world,
where elephants climb trees and tigers ride camels."

He stuck his head into the hole to show Petunia.
"When *her* head is in the hole," he chuckled to himself,
"I will grab her neck and . . . ."
"Ouch! Ouch! Ouch!" he suddenly shrieked.
Backing out, he ran foolishly in circles
with a swarm of angry bees about his head.
He had put his nose into their nest!

Petunia chased the bees with her wings.
"There, dear friend," she said. "Stop running round and round.
Or run the other way. You make me dizzy.
Tell me, do the bees come from the other side of the world?"
"Don't stand there asking silly questions," growled Raccoon.
"Don't you see my head is all swollen?
Let's run before the bees come back."

After Raccoon had cooled his head in a spring,
the two went on along the forest path.
Petunia picked leaves here and there
while Raccoon, hungrier than ever, looked about
for a proper way to trap the goose.
"THERE, the forest wishing stone," he suddenly cried,
pointing to a big rock with a smaller one on top.
"If you kiss the big rock at the bottom twenty times
and make twenty wishes, they will all come true."
"I don't think I can find twenty wishes," said Petunia,
"but I will try. Will you try, too?"
"I have only one wish," answered Raccoon, gritting his teeth.

Raccoon showed Petunia where she must kiss the rock (low, very low at the bottom), and he climbed to the top to push the small rock onto her head. As he pushed and pushed, the rock rocked like a rocking chair. But, instead of rolling toward Petunia, it rolled back toward Raccoon—

and pushed him down to the forest floor.
His shrieks brought Petunia quickly to his aid.
"What have you done again, and what are you trying to do?"
she cried, seeing him walking on three legs.
"Ouch, my paw, that rock," muttered Raccoon.
"I made my wish, but it did not come true.
But it will *next time*," he added angrily.

After rubbing his paw and walking for awhile,
Raccoon forgot his pain and looked again
for a trick that would not fail.

"I have it—a seesaw,"
he cried presently, when
he saw a plank which
had been forgotten under
a tree by lumbermen.
The plank lay across
a stone with one end up.
"What's a seesaw?"
asked Petunia. "A very
amusing game," answered
Raccoon. "Let's play it."

He sat Petunia on the smaller end
of the plank, under a low branch
of the tree. Then he climbed up
to a higher branch above the
other end. "Now, watch me,"
he said. "I'll jump down onto
the plank and you will go up,
up, up. . . ." Then he added to
himself, "And you will hit the
branch above, bang! and be
all muddled up."
Raccoon jumped,

but the plank yielded only a little
and sprang right up, throwing *him* back to the high branch
which *he* hit with *his* head . . . BANG!
"What happened?" shouted Petunia. "I didn't go up at all!"
"I did, didn't you see, you silly goose?" grunted Raccoon, rubbing
his head with one paw while he held on to the branch with the other.
"That's the wrong sort of seesaw.
Let's go find something else."

Raccoon was so tired and hungry now,
he only wanted something to eat. Anything!
The two walked on down the path. It led past a farm
which stood in the meadow at the edge of the forest.
"I think I smell raspberry jam," said Petunia.
"Strawberry," said Raccoon. "And, when all is said,
there is nothing better than strawberry jam in the morning.
I see it there in that wire box behind the barn."
Without stopping to think why strawberry jam should be there,
Raccoon rushed into the box. The door snapped shut.
The box was a trap.

"Oh, it's the end of me, Petunia," cried Raccoon.
"Look, the farmer has seen us; he is coming. Oh, Petunia."
But Petunia was already trying to open the door.
She shook it every possible way, tugging at it from all sides,
while the farmer was getting nearer and nearer.
Just as he reached them,
Petunia opened the door,
and Raccoon rushed out, free.

They fled through the meadow with the farmer after them.
But they soon lost sight of him.
He could neither run like a raccoon nor fly like a goose.
It was only in the middle of the forest
that Petunia and Raccoon stopped to rest.

"Dearest Petunia," said Raccoon, "I must tell you something.
Do you know why I asked you to come into the woods?"
"Your aunt!" cried Petunia. "Your aunt, we forgot her!"
"Oh, well . . . never mind," said Racoon. "What I must say is
thank you, dearest Petunia, for saving my life.
From now on, I will be your truest friend, for ever and ever."
They chattered happily all the way back to Petunia's farm.
When they parted company at the gate, Petunia said,
"Really, Raccoon, it's the loveliest walk I have ever had,
even if we never saw your aunt."
"Good-by, Petunia," said Raccoon. "I love you."